For my favorite pirate, CeCe, and for Jon Scieszka, without whom this book would not exist. —I. F.

For Rowan and Alice, from your aunt Budgie! —B. B.

BLOOMSBURY CHILDREN'S BOOKS
Bloomsbury Publishing Inc., part of Bloomsbury Publishing Plc
1385 Broadway, New York, NY 10018

BLOOMSBURY, BLOOMSBURY CHILDREN'S BOOKS, and the Diana logo are trademarks of Bloomsbury Publishing Plc

First published in the United States of America in March 2020 by Bloomsbury Children's Books

Text copyright © 2020 by Isaac Fitzgerald
Illustrations copyright © 2020 by Brigette Barrager

Bloomsbury books may be purchased for business or promotional use. For information on bulk purchases please contact Macmillan Corporate and Premium Sales Department at specialmarkets@macmillan.com

Library of Congress Cataloging-in-Publication Data
Names: Fitzgerald, Isaac, author. | Barrager, Brigette, illustrator.
Title: How to be a pirate / by Isaac Fitzgerald ; illustrated by Brigette Barrager.
Description: New York : Bloomsbury, 2020.
Summary: Told by the neighborhood boys that she cannot be a pirate,
CeCe seeks reassurance from her grandfather who knows about boats and has tattoos.
Identifiers: LCCN 2019019158 (print) | LCCN 2019021853 (e-book)
ISBN 978-1-68119-778-4 (hardcover) • ISBN 978-1-5476-0005-2 (e-book) • ISBN 978-1-5476-0006-9 (e-PDF)
Subjects: | CYAC: Pirates—Fiction. | Grandfathers—Fiction. | Tattooing—Fiction.
Classification: LCC PZ7.1.F573 Ho 2020 (print) | LCC PZ7.1.F573 (e-book) | DDC [E]—dc23
LC record available at https://lccn.loc.gov/2019019158

Art created with pencil, colored pencil, and ink washes composited in Photoshop
Typeset in Blueprint MT Sd
Book design by Danielle Ceccolini
Printed in China by Leo Paper Products, Heshan, Guangdong
2 4 6 8 10 9 7 5 3 1

All papers used by Bloomsbury Publishing Plc are natural, recyclable products made from wood grown in well-managed forests.
The manufacturing processes conform to the environmental regulations of the country of origin.

To find out more about our authors and books visit www.bloomsbury.com and sign up for our newsletters.

HOW TO BE A PIRATE

ISAAC FITZGERALD

illustrated by BRIGETTE BARRAGER

BLOOMSBURY
CHILDREN'S BOOKS
NEW YORK LONDON OXFORD NEW DELHI SYDNEY

CeCe was mad. Who were those boys to say she couldn't be a pirate?
They had probably never even been on a boat.

But CeCe knew somebody who had . . .

"What's it like to be a pirate?"

"Why do you think I know anything about that?" Grandpa asked. "And tell me—why do you want to know about pirates?"

CeCe took a deep breath.

"Because . . . ," she said, "the boys are pretending
to be pirates and I wanted to play too—I even brought
my sword! But they said 'you can't be a pirate' and
what if they're right? I don't know how to be one.
But maybe you do? Because of your ship!
I know pirates have tattoos—so I was
thinking maybe you know all about them.
Can you teach me?"

"So, you want to know about pirates, eh?" asked Grandpa.
"Well, I guess the first thing a pirate needs to be is . . .

BRAVE!

A pirate seeks out adventure and isn't afraid of obstacles ahead."

"What else?" asked CeCe.

"You have to be . . .

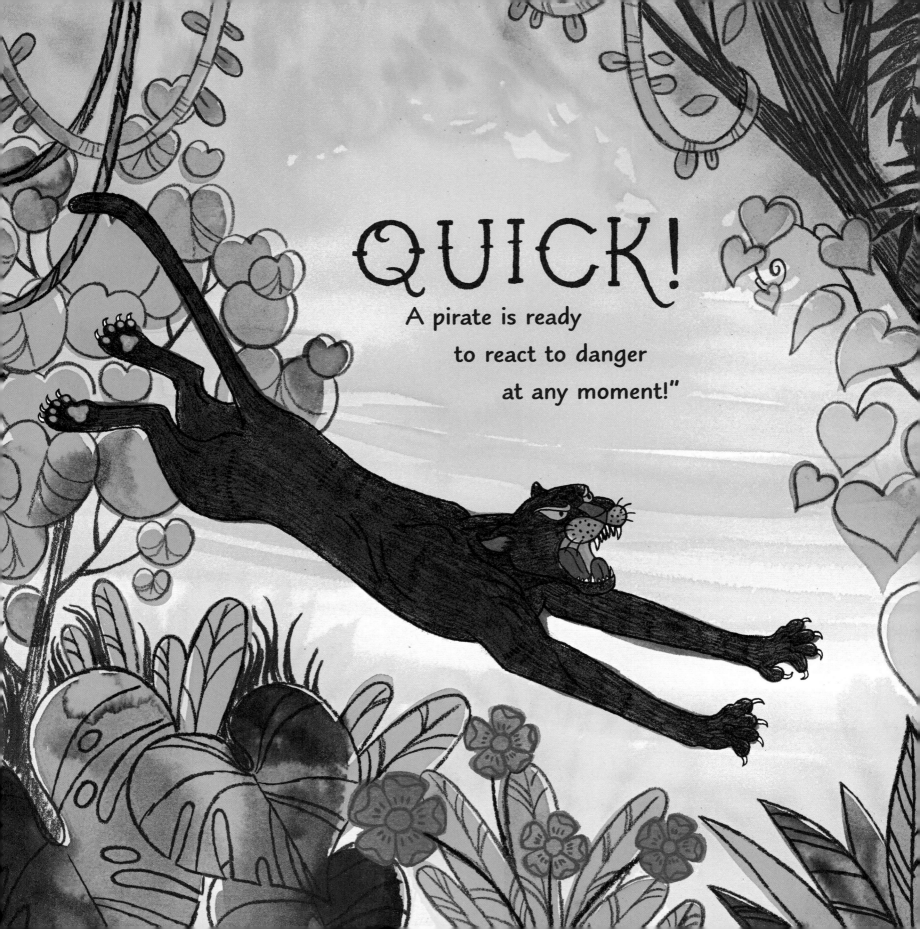

QUICK!

A pirate is ready
to react to danger
at any moment!"

"Another one?" CeCe asked.

"It isn't all about danger, though . . . ," whispered Grandpa. "A pirate knows how to have . . .

FUN!

"More!" yelled CeCe.

"Another thing a pirate
must be is . . ."

INDEPENDENT!

Having a good crew is important, but at the end of the day a
pirate must face her problems on her own!"

"But do you know the most important quality a pirate should have?" asked Grandpa. "It's something even more important than being brave or quick, knowing how to have fun, or even being independent . . ."

"Is it treasure?" CeCe asked. "Or cannons?"

"The most important thing a person can have, pirate or not, is . . .

LOVE!

CeCe ran, her feet swift and her heart strong.